Pom and Pim

Lena and Olof Landström

Pom and Pim

GECKO PRESS

Pom and Pim are going out.

It's warm. The sun is shining.
What luck!

Ouch!

Bad luck.

Money!

What luck!

Pom buys an ice cream.

Pim has a taste.

The ice cream is good. Pom eats it quickly.

Pom gets a tummy ache.

That's bad luck.

Pom has to lie down.

The balloon!

What luck!

Pom and Pim go back outside.

The balloon bounces beautifully.

Bad luck.
The balloon's broken.

Pom has an idea.

A raincoat for Pim!

Now it's raining.

What luck!

This edition first published in 2014 by Gecko Press
PO Box 9335, Marion Square, Wellington 6141, New Zealand
info@geckopress.com

Distributed in New Zealand by Random House NZ
Distributed in Australia by Scholastic Australia
Distributed in the United Kingdom by Bounce Sales & Marketing

First American edition published in 2014 by Gecko Press USA,
an imprint of Gecko Press Ltd.
Distributed in the United States and Canada by
Lerner Publishing Group, Inc.
241 First Avenue North
Minneapolis, MN 55401 USA
www.lernerbooks.com

A catalog record for this book is available from the US Library of Congress.
Copyright © Lilla Piratförlaget AB, 2012
Original title: *Pom och Pim*

The cost of this translation was defrayed by a subsidy from the Swedish Arts Council,
gratefully acknowledged.

This edition © Gecko Press Ltd 2014
Reprinted 2014

A catalogue record for this book is available from the National Library of New Zealand

Text by Lena Landström
Illustrations by Olof Landström
Translated by Julia Marshall
Edited by Penelope Todd
Typeset by Vida & Luke Kelly, New Zealand
Printed in China by Everbest Printing Co Ltd, an accredited ISO 14001 & FSC
certified printer

ISBN hardback: 978-1-877579-66-0
ISBN paperback: 978-1-877579-88-2

For more curiously good books, visit www.geckopress.com